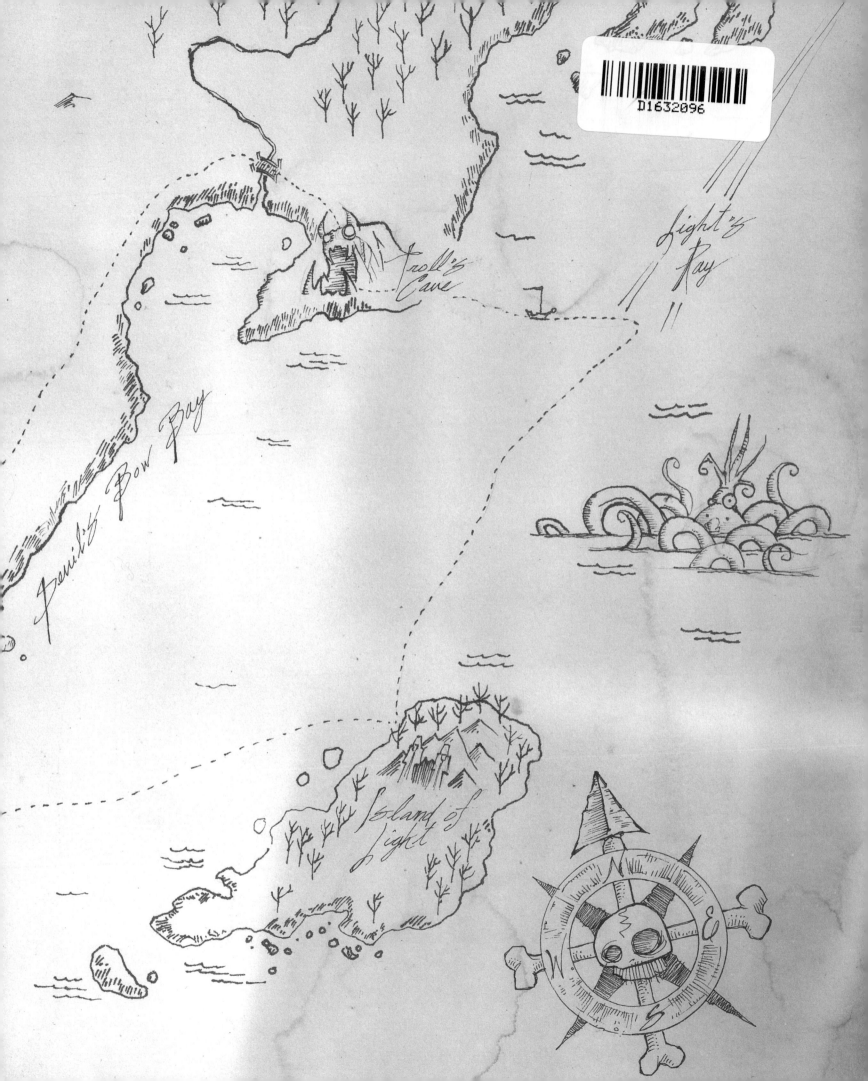

Troll's Cave

Light's Bay

Devil's Bow Bay

Island of Light

Little Jordan Ray's Muddy Spud

Gris Grimly

For my mum and dad, who raised me well.

"Baby Tattoo," "Baby Tattoo Books" and logo are trademarks of Baby Tattoo Books.

ISBN 0-9729388-6-9
Library of Congress Control Number: 2004098240

First Edition

10 9 8 7 6 5 4 3 2 1

Published by Baby Tattoo Books
Van Nuys, California
www.babytattoo.com

Designed by eric@pixelectomy

Manufactured in China

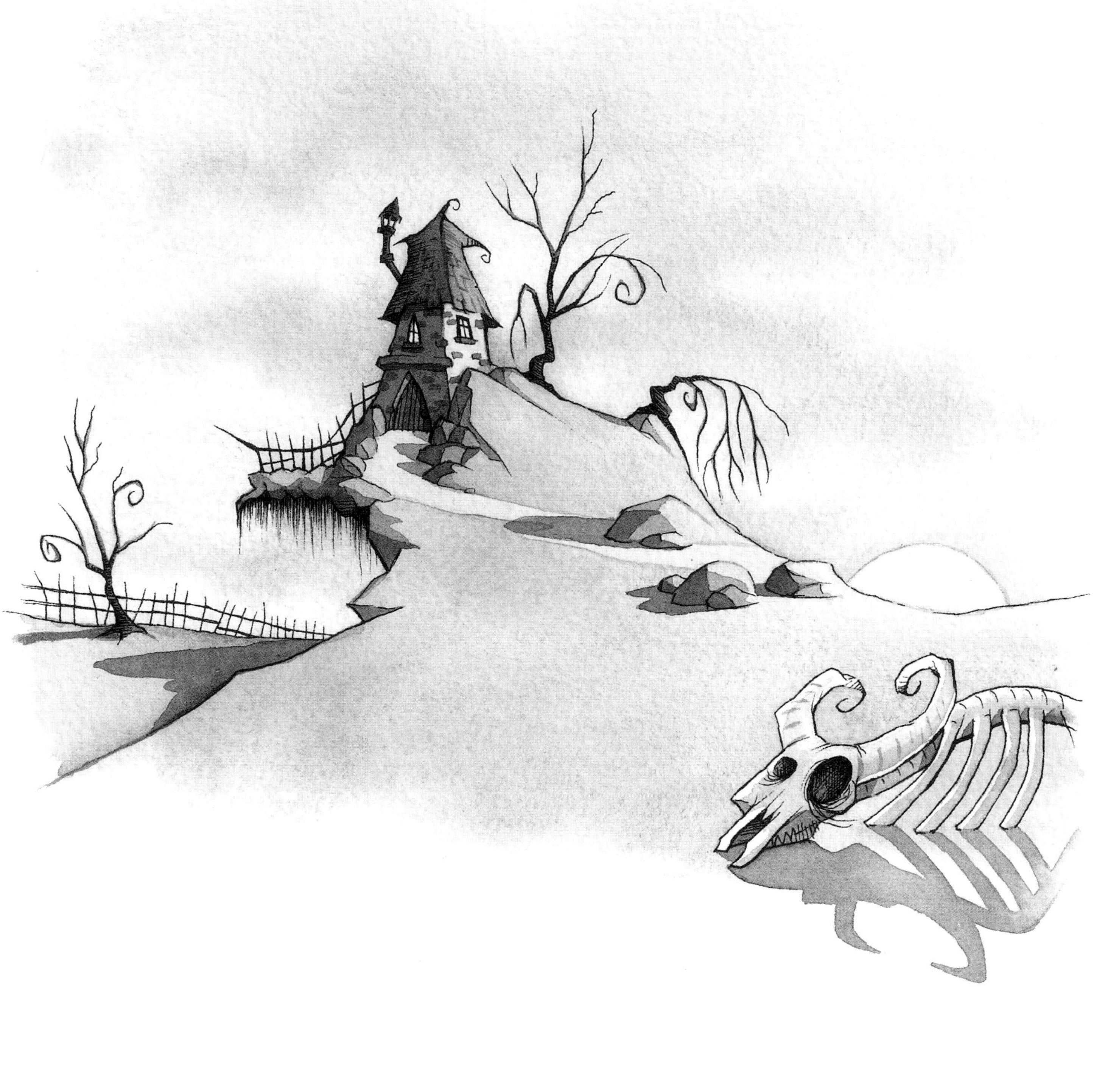

The farmlands were cruel and plagued with a drought.
The ground was stone cold and the sun never came out.

A family of three sat still at their table.
They had rats in their floor and bats in their gable.
Their cupboards were empty and they had no heat.
Their harvest had withered and so had their meat.
All that they had was a large lumpy spud
that they'd found in the field all covered with mud.

Little Jordan Ray was a scrawny young lad.
At the age of nine, he worked hard for his dad.
"It's up to you son, to bring home the pay.
I trust you'll do well on this October day.
Take this spud to the village and barter it off.
Accept the best offer and don't be too soft."

His dear sweet mum, with her worried caress,
expressed to her son her concerns and distress,
"Don't diddle daddle as you go on your way.
Don't talk to strangers, and be back today."

Little Jordan Ray went away with the spud in a sack.
"You can trust me," he said. "I'll hurry back."

He hiked along, down dusty rock trails,
through dry barren pastures...

...and over steep hills.

He reached a stone wall with a peasant beneath,
who was missing his legs and most of his teeth.
His voice was gruff and came out with a croak.
But nevertheless, he eventually spoke,
"Excuse me lad, can you spare me a pound,
or maybe a shilling if one can be found."

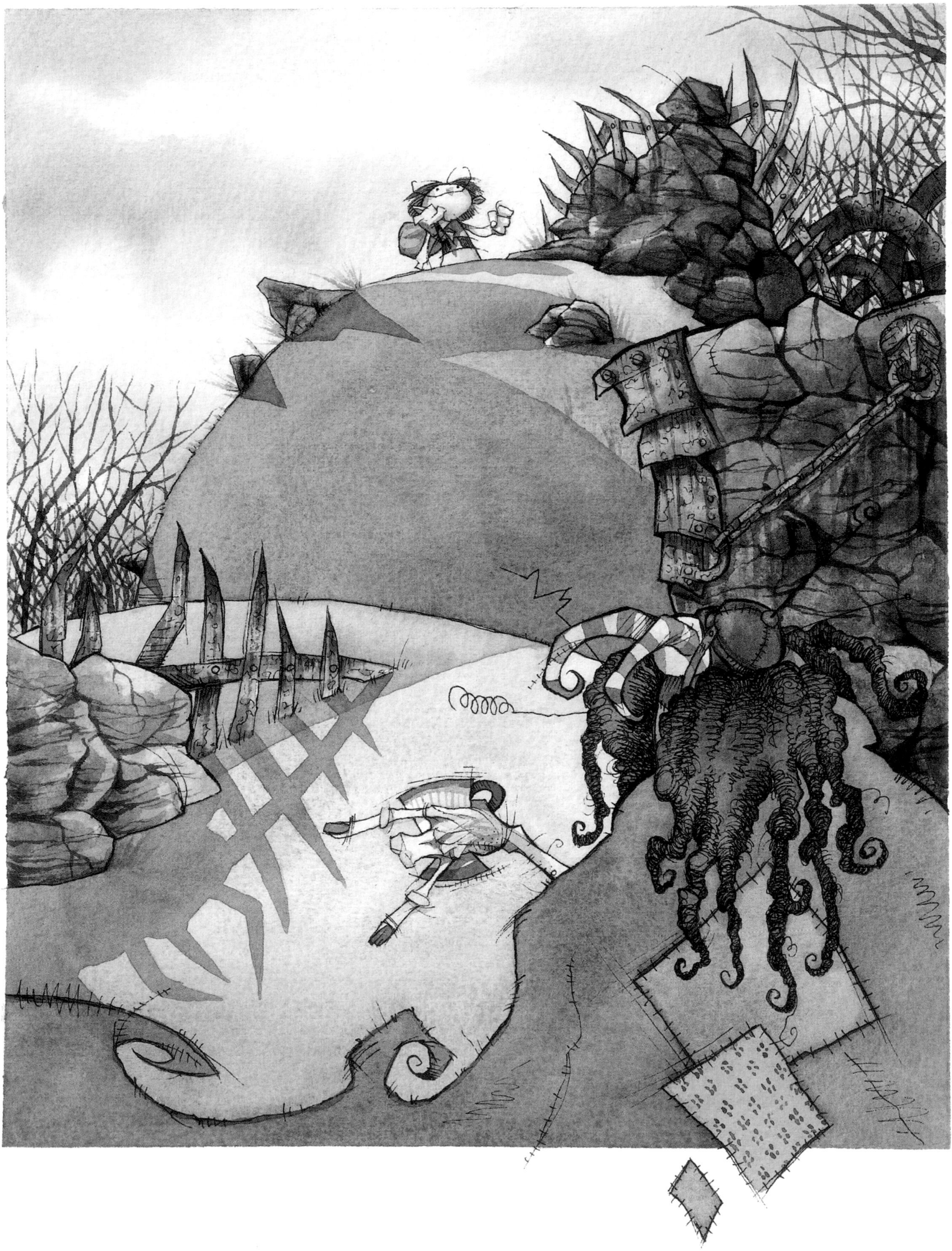

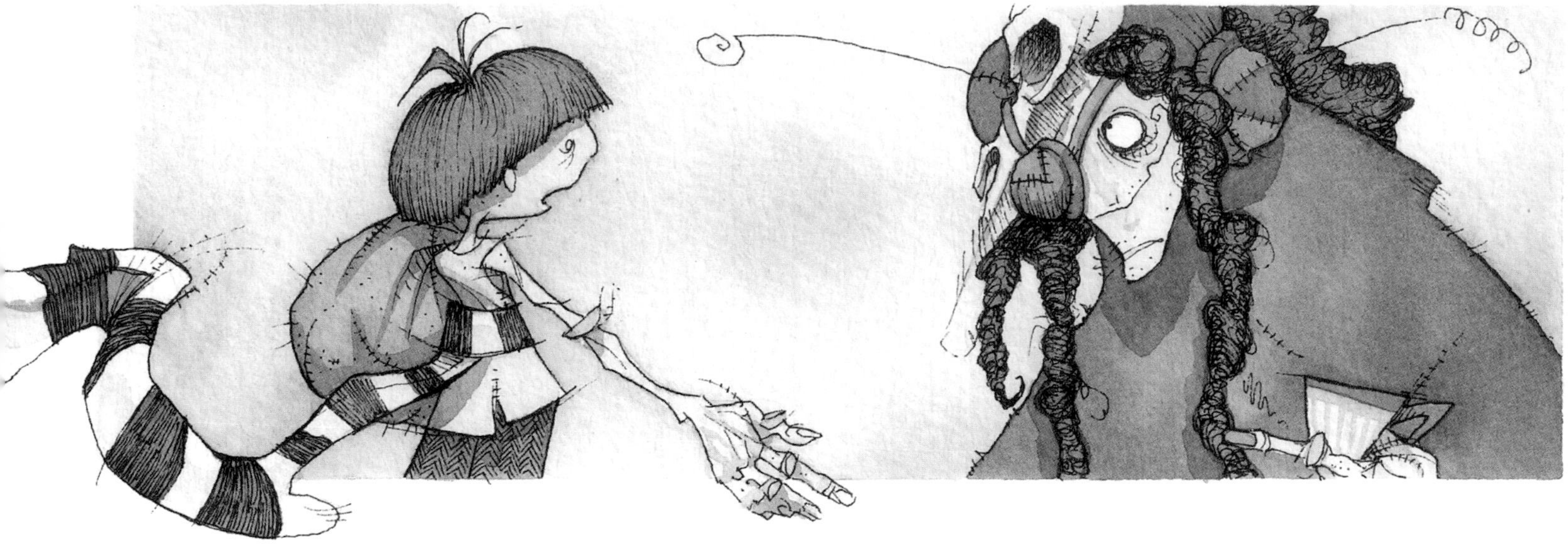

Little Jordan Ray was bright, but a little too kind;
his charity would often cloud up his mind.
He turned to the man and let out a sigh,
"I'm sorry sir, I will not tell a lie.
All I have is a spud in the sack on my back.
Shillings and pounds are something I lack."

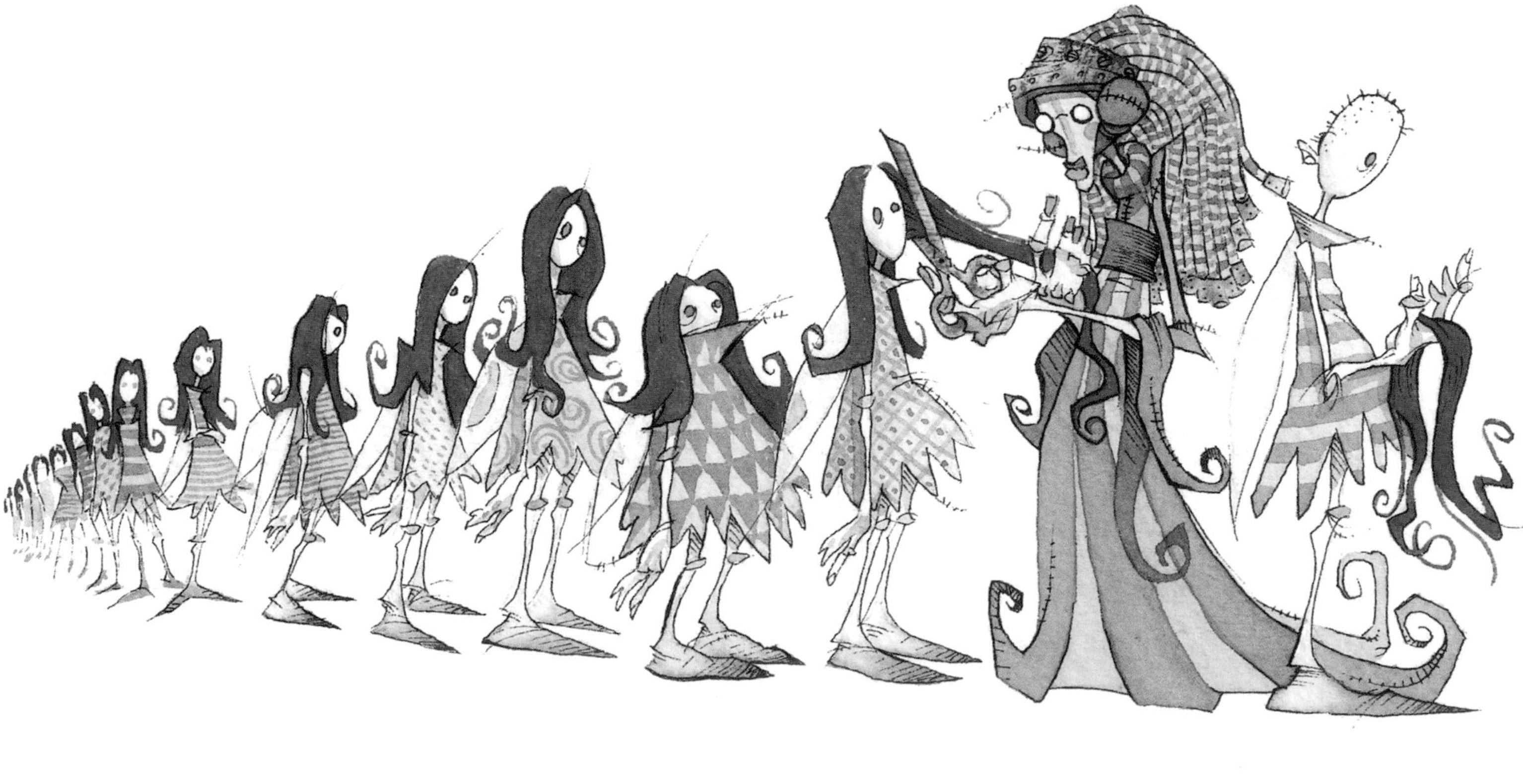

"My apologies lad, but I have no need for a spud.

Just a single spud all covered with mud.

But one thing I can use is Sergeant Jock's socks.

These mystical socks can make the lame walk.

Ten zillion fairies gave up their own hair

to be woven together to make this rare pair.

A mad hare wears the pair of stockings this day.

I believe he lives on Devil's Bow Bay.

I can't go myself, for I am too weak.

But if you bring me the socks, I'll grant what ye seek."

Little Jordan Ray pondered this thought with a hunch,
I could fetch him his socks and get back by lunch.

If I trade off the spud, I won't have it to sell.
But if the man tells the truth, he'll pay me quite well.

The man said he would give me a price that is right.
If I then hurry home, I'll get there tonight.

He agreed with the man to go find the hare.
He gave him his word and made a pinky swear.

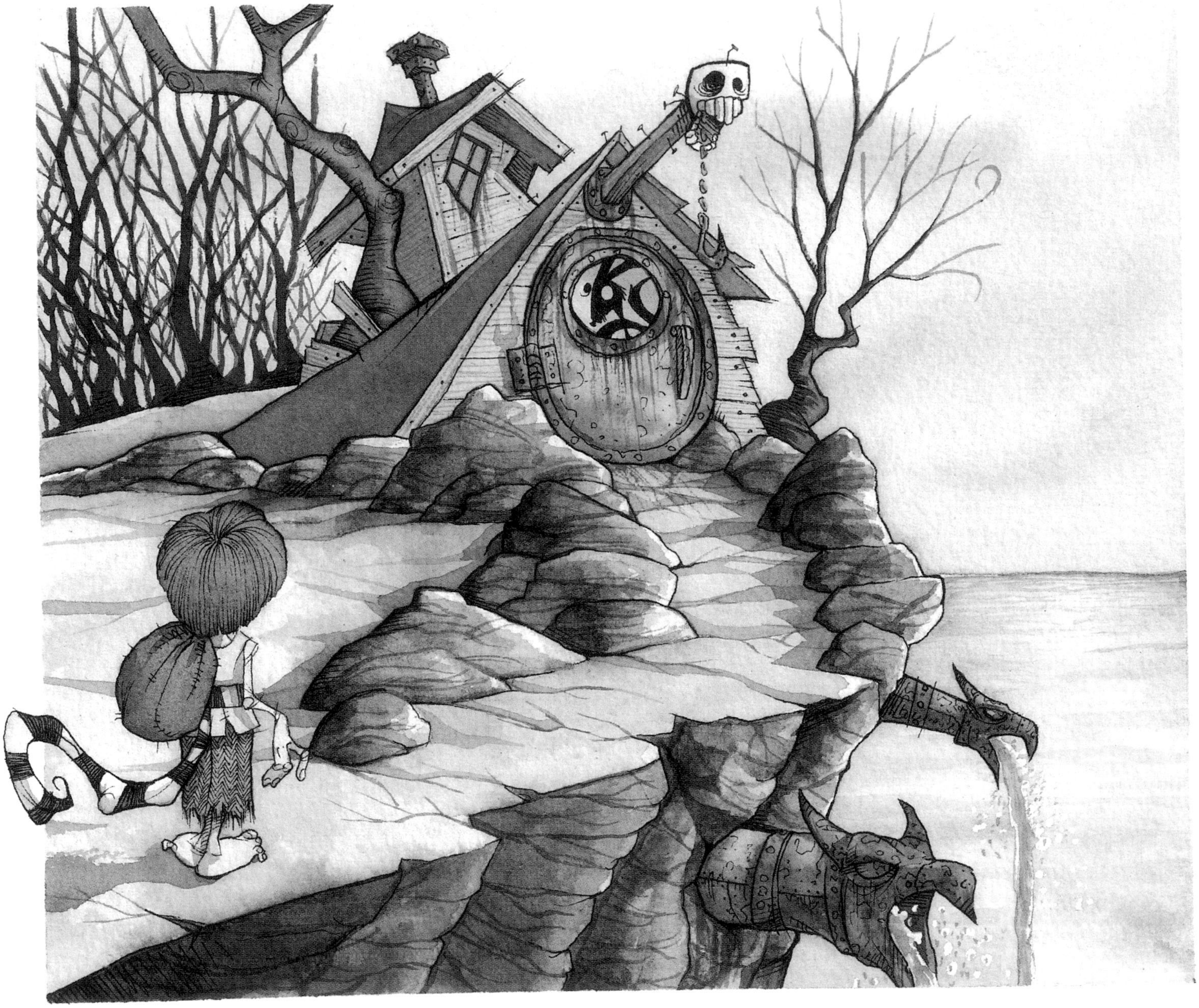

Little Jordan Ray set off to Devil's Bow Bay
to retrieve Sergeant Jock's socks on this October day.
The distance was long, but covered in short.
The hare was having brunch in a little wood fort.

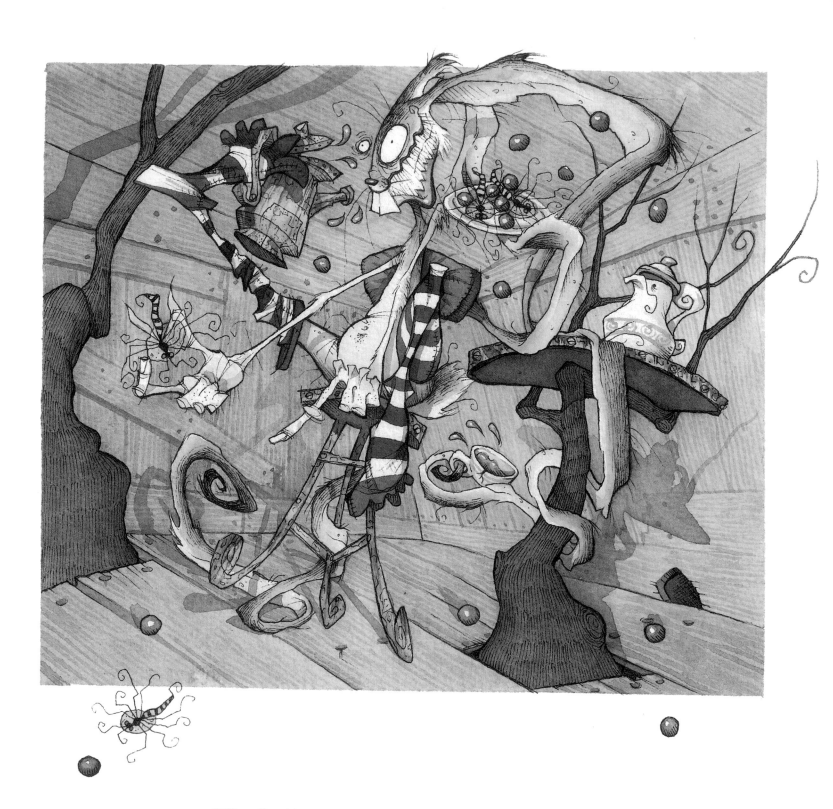

"Can I offer you a wonderful waspberry torte?
Or maybe a chocolate-covered toad wart,"
said the mad hare, wearing the rare socks.

"Thank you Mr. Hare, but my business is short.
I have no time to eat a single sweet torte.
I have here a mud-covered spud from the range
and all that I ask is your socks in exchange."

"My apologies, lad, but I have no need for a spud.
Just a single spud all covered with mud.
But one thing I can use is this big blue balloon.
It defies gravity 'cause it was made by the moon.
My ears are too long and they drag on the floor.
But tied to the balloon they'll soar ever more.
It's tied to the wrist of a grumpy old troll
who lives on the coast in a dumpy old hole.
He feeds on rabbits, and I think I am one.
But if you bring me the balloon, our deal will be done."

Little Jordan Ray took off with no delay
to retrieve the big blue balloon on this October day.
He found the troll in his hole by the coast.
He was beginning his lunch with a customary toast.

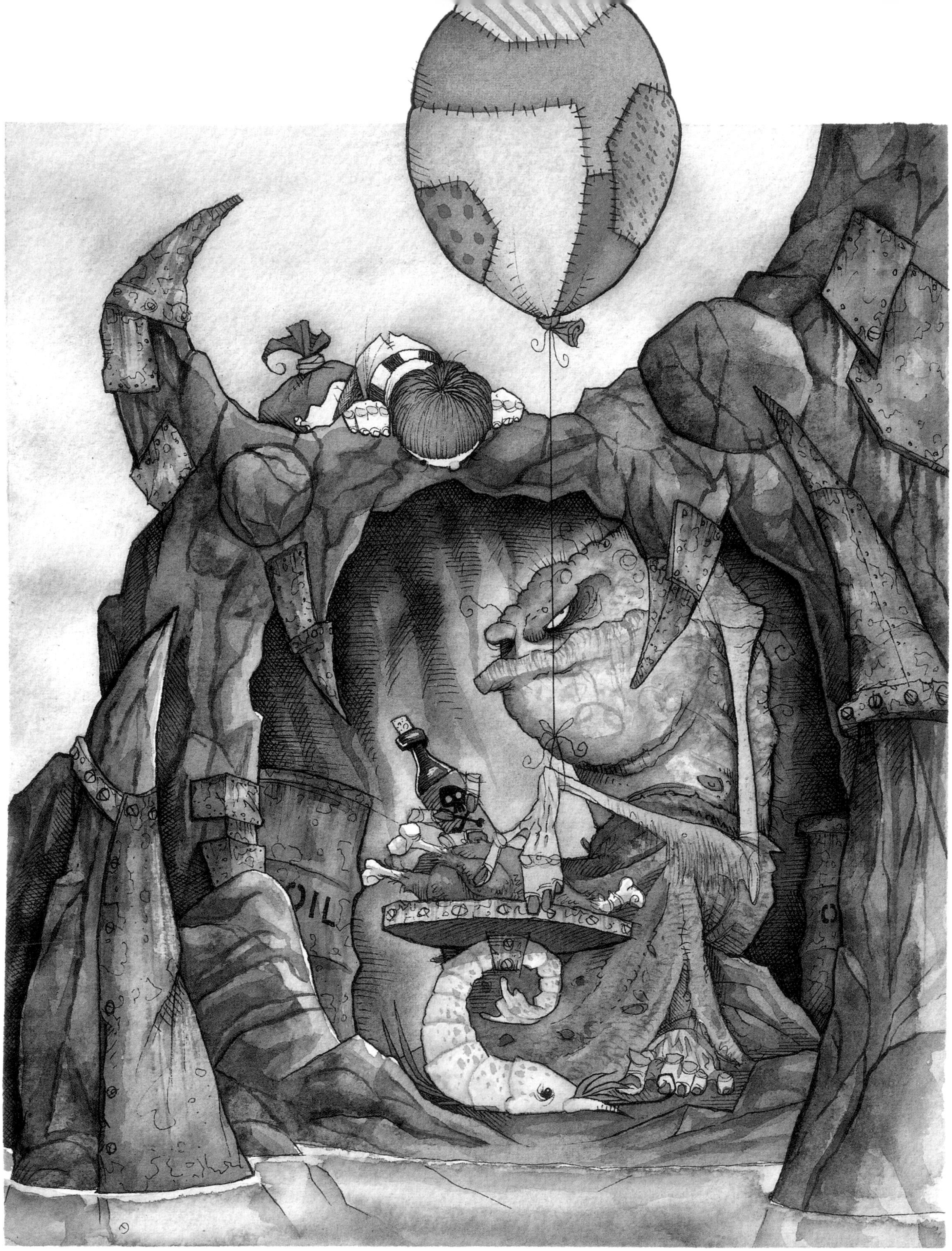
OIL

"What draws you lingering during my toast?
Do you smell the aroma of rabbit rump roast?"
scolded the grumpy old troll, holding the balloon.

"I'm sorry Mr. Troll, I don't mean to pry.
But I noticed your balloon as I hap'd to pass by.
I have here a mud-covered spud from the range
and all that I ask is your balloon in exchange."

"My apologies lad, but I have no need for a spud.
Just a single spud all covered with mud.
But one thing I can use is Triton's pearl teeth.
An oyster now has them in the sea beneath.
The teeth that I have are rotted clear through.
It makes rabbit rump roast a challenge to chew.
You can take my boat and sail out to the sun.
A ray of light will then point out the one.
I would get it myself, only I fear the sea.
But if you bring me the teeth, you can trade with me."

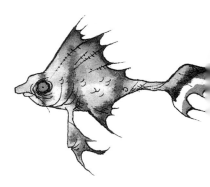

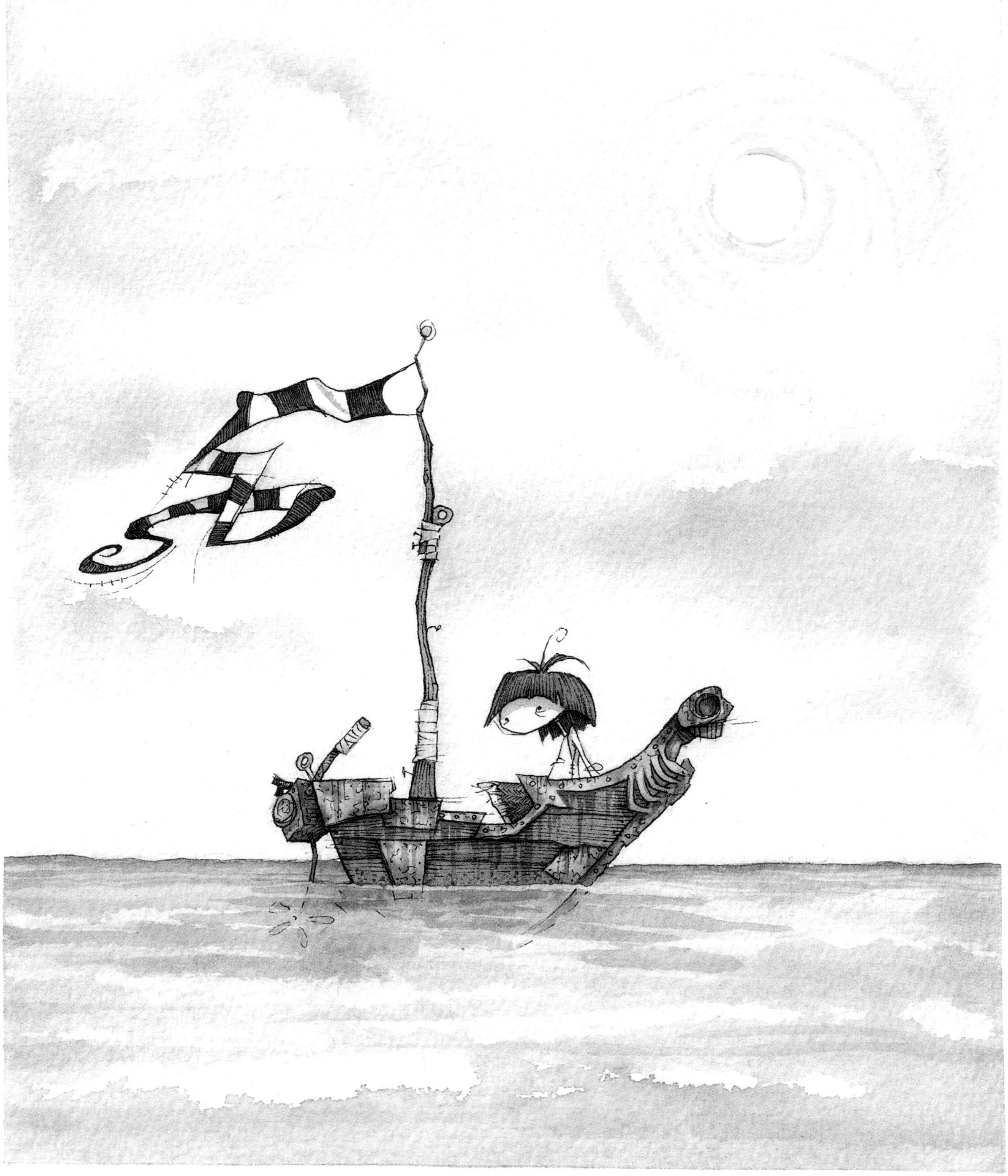

Little Jordan Ray sailed towards the light's ray
to retrieve Triton's pearl teeth on this October day.
The sunbeam trickled down to an oyster underneath.
He was having his tea with his pearly pearl teeth.

"Who calls the sun to shoot light in my eyes?
What a rude interruption as I eat crawfish pies,"
the oyster replied, squinting his eyes as he cried.

"I'm sorry to disturb you as you snap at your snack.
But I bring you a gift in the sack on my back.
I have here a mud-covered spud from the range
and all that I ask is your teeth in exchange."

"My apologies lad, but I have no need for a spud.
Just a single spud all covered with mud.
But one thing I can use is the orb of King Earl.
For I will be worthless if I give you each pearl.
The orb is speckled with priceless red rubies.
They were taken from the souls of three hundred babies.
The orb is now the possession of Sir Lucien the Knight.
He awaits a fierce battle on the Island of Light.
I'm not fond of the light so I must stay beneath.
But if you bring me the orb, you can have the teeth."

Little Jordan Ray let the sun's light guide his way
to retrieve King Earl's orb on this October day.
There, on the Island of Light, stood Lucien the Knight.
He was entirely too busy to take time for a bite.

"My apologies young boy, I am too busy today.
I have no time to partake in the games that you play,"
the knight on the Island of Light recited with spite.

"I am not here to play games but to trade and to barter.
You must take a pause from your efforts at martyr.
I have here a mud-covered spud from the range
and all that I ask is the orb in exchange."

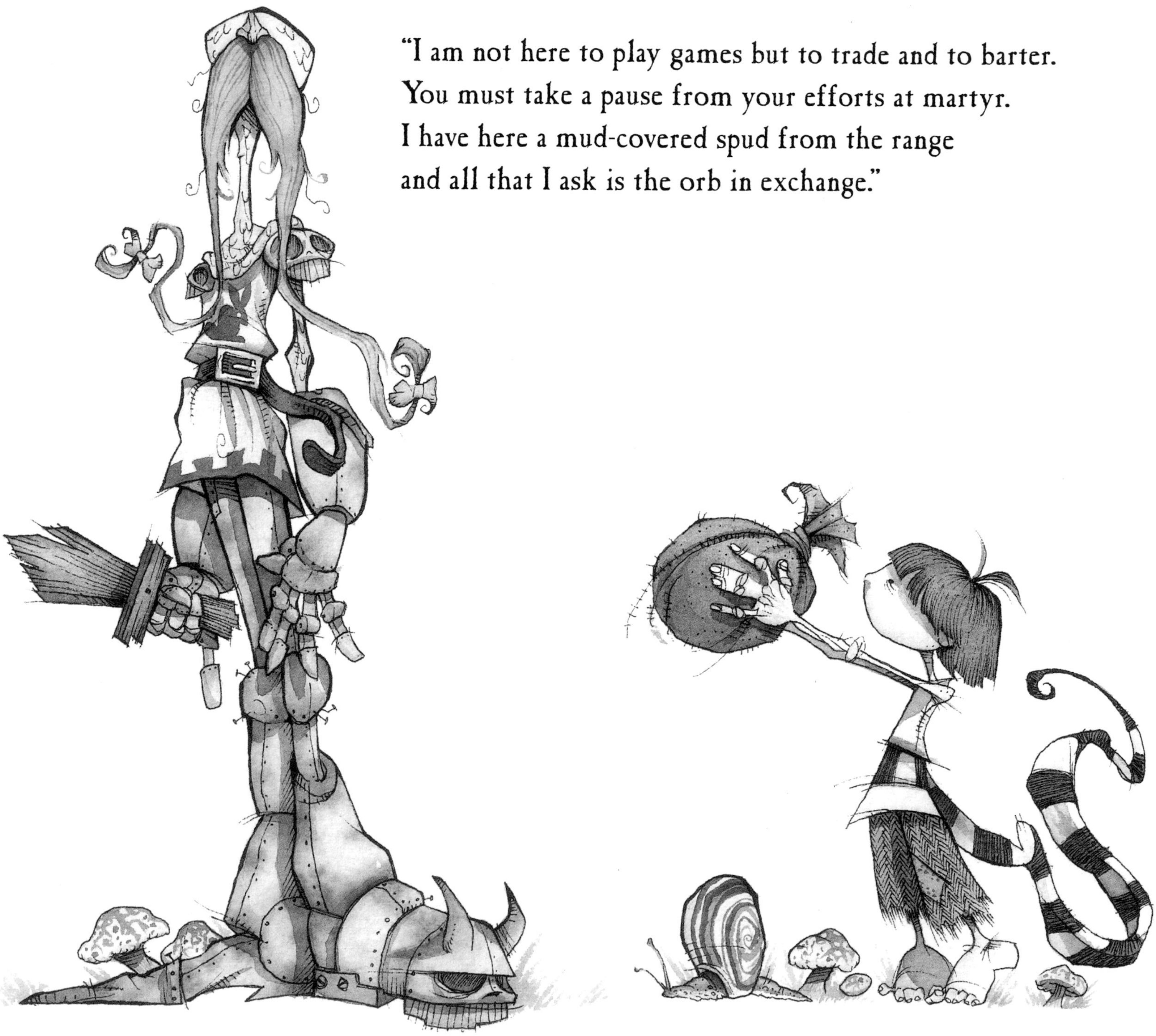

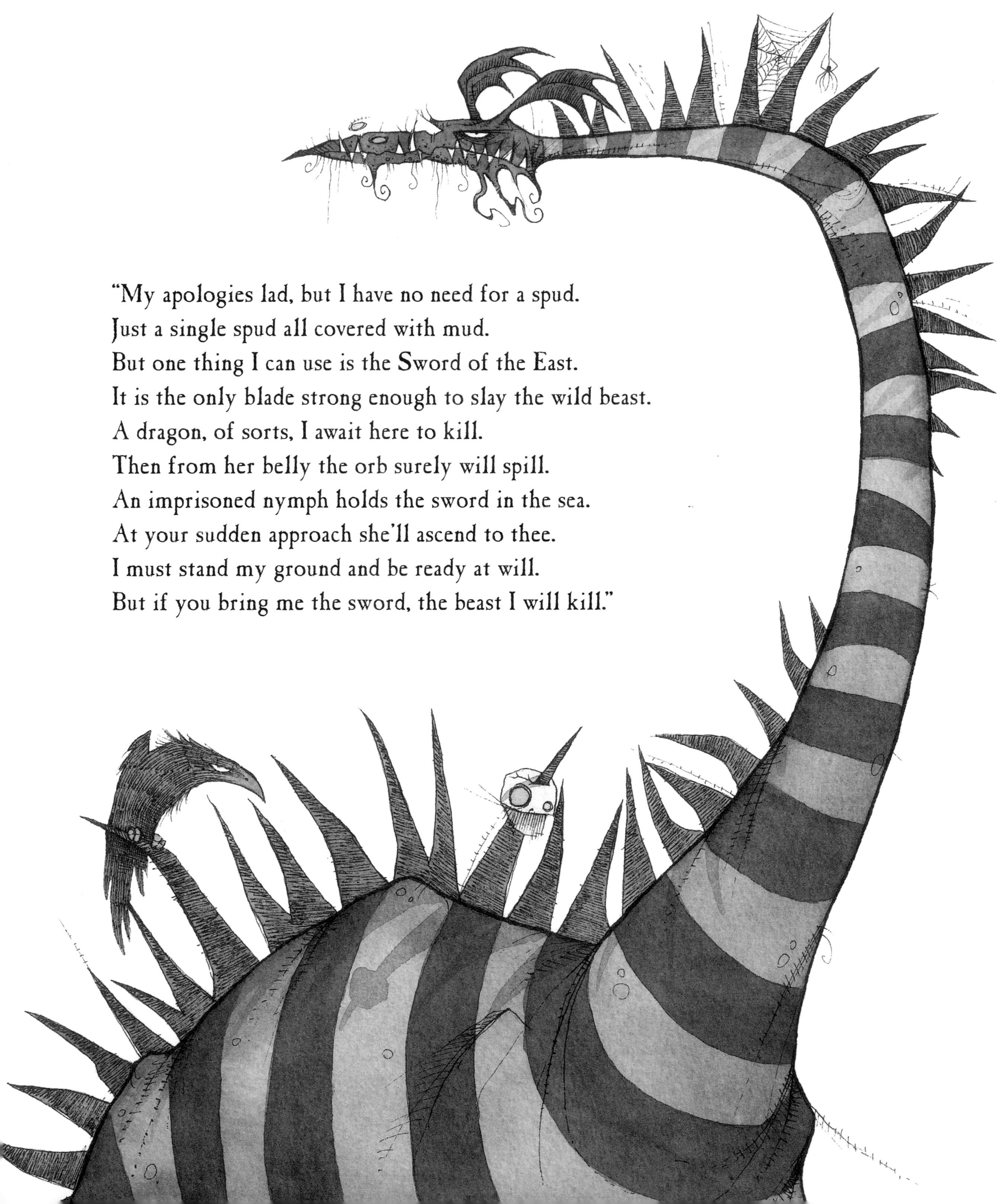

"My apologies lad, but I have no need for a spud.
Just a single spud all covered with mud.
But one thing I can use is the Sword of the East.
It is the only blade strong enough to slay the wild beast.
A dragon, of sorts, I await here to kill.
Then from her belly the orb surely will spill.
An imprisoned nymph holds the sword in the sea.
At your sudden approach she'll ascend to thee.
I must stand my ground and be ready at will.
But if you bring me the sword, the beast I will kill."

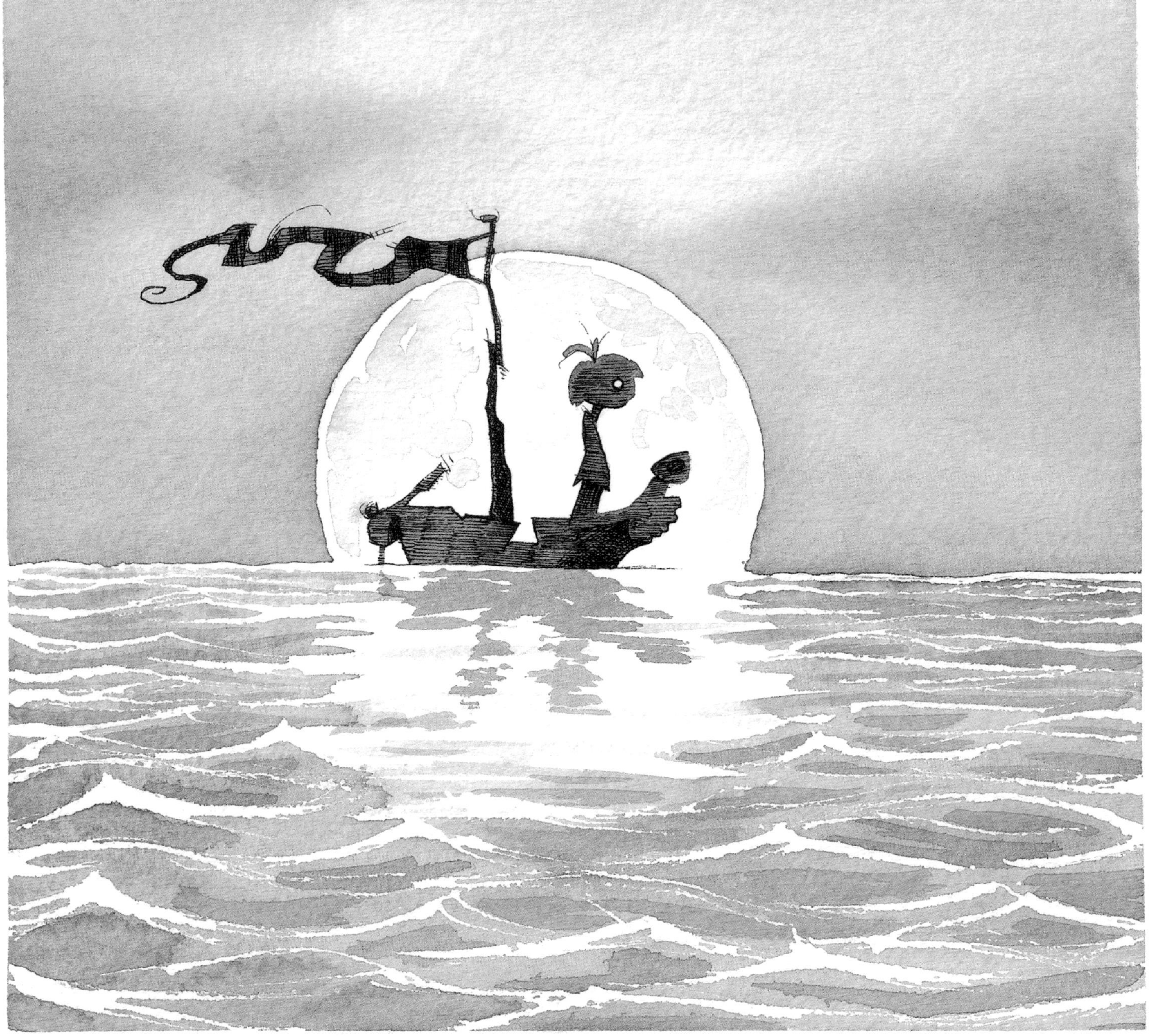

Little Jordan Ray sailed out on the wide waterway
to retrieve the Sword of the East on this October day.
With a watery spray, the nymph arose with the sword.
Her wrists were in shackles and chained to a board.

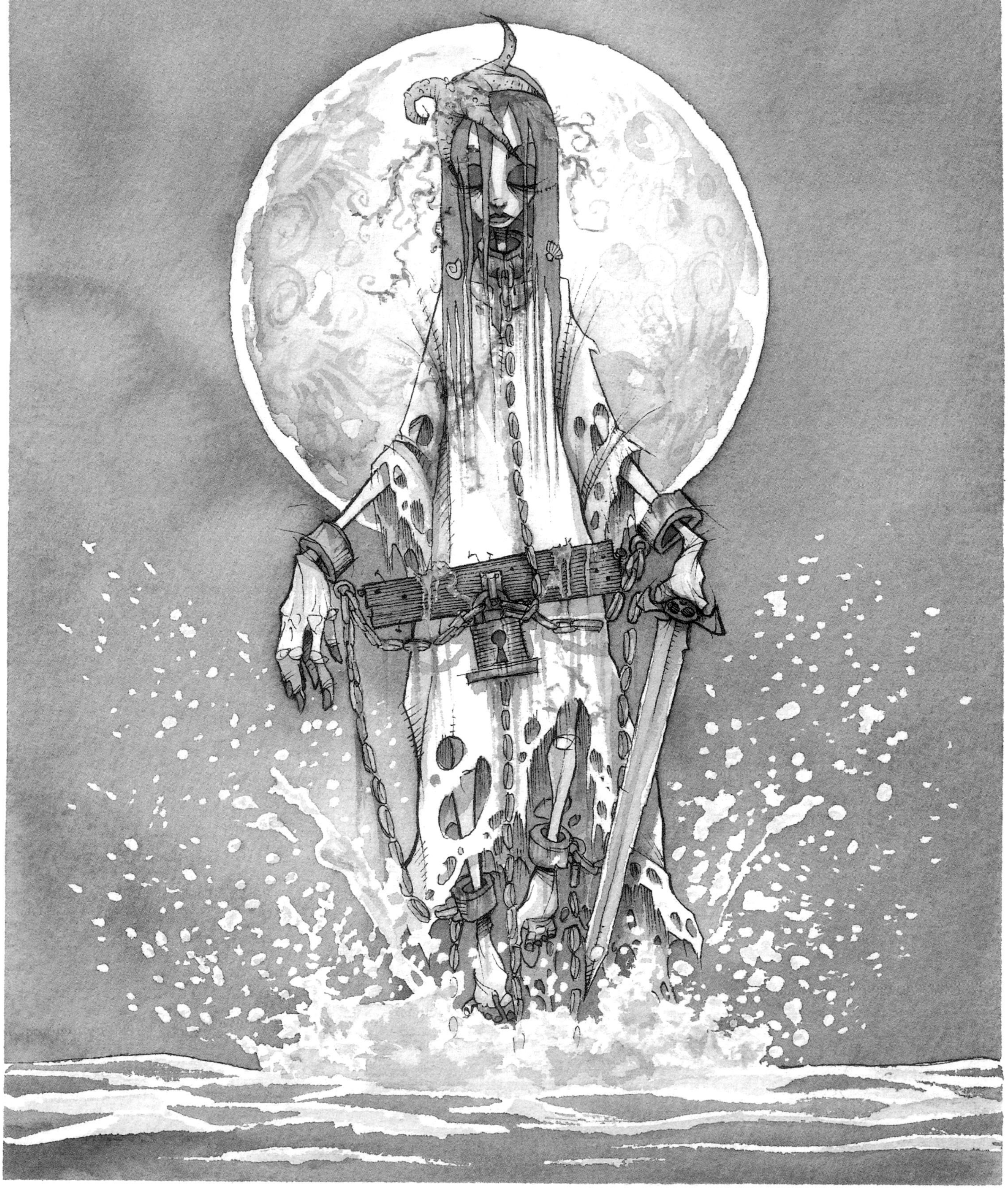

"You have disturbed my dinner of water and bread.
For this selfish act I should chop off your head."
Said the gaunt water nymph hauntingly blunt.

"I am sorry to bring you up out of your kelp,
but Sir Lucien the Knight is in need of your help.
I have here a mud-covered spud from the range
and all that I ask is your sword in exchange."

"My apologies lad, but I have no need for a spud.
Just a single spud all covered in mud.
But one thing I can use is the key to my lock.
I've been a prisoner for centuries, chained to this rock.
All that I ask is to one day be free.
A water nymph should be able to swim the whole sea.
The key's high in an oak tree that sprouts from the shore,
in an egg of a griffin, according to lore.
I am but a prisoner, chained up by my Lord.
But if you bring me the key, I will grant you the sword."

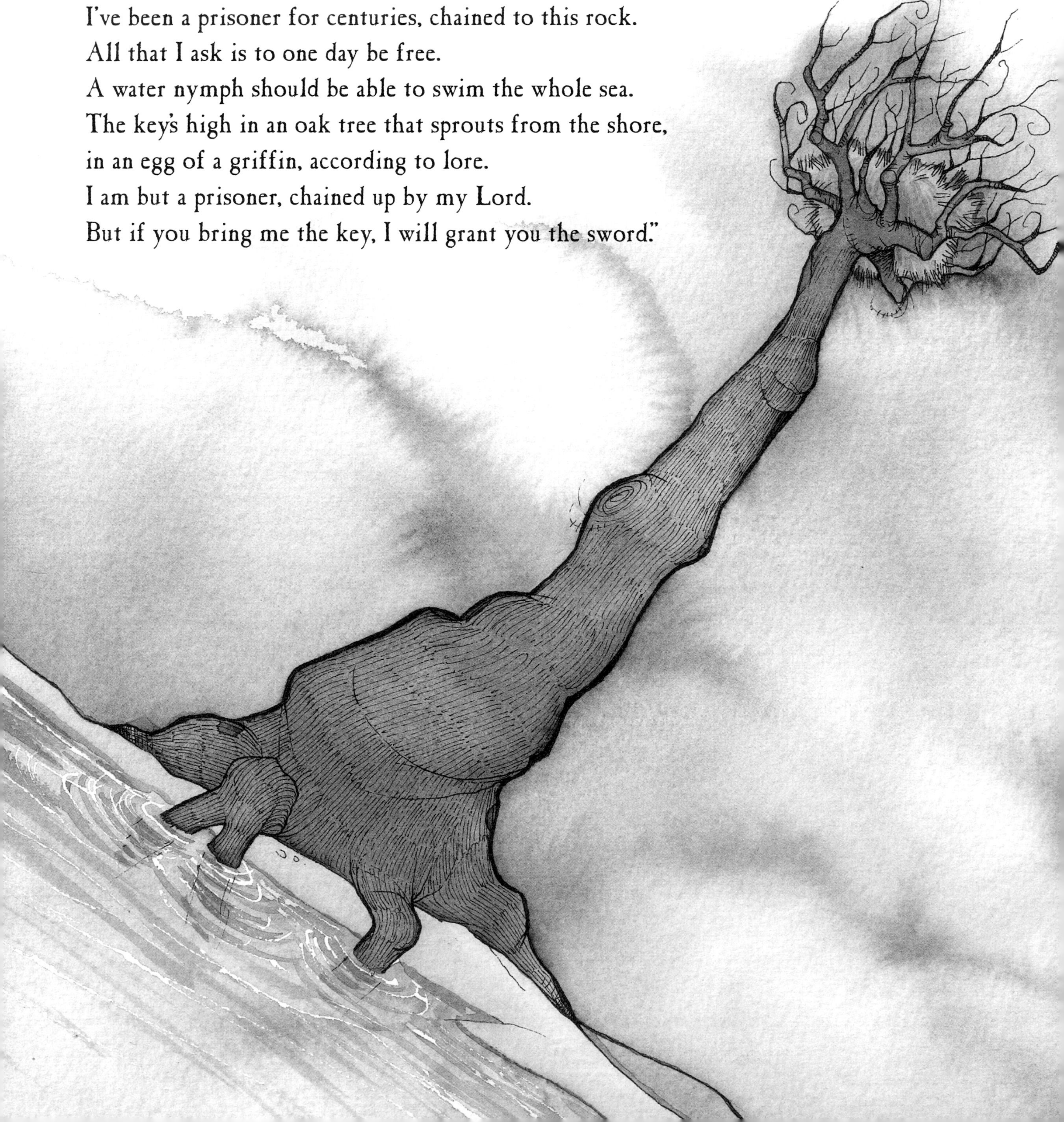

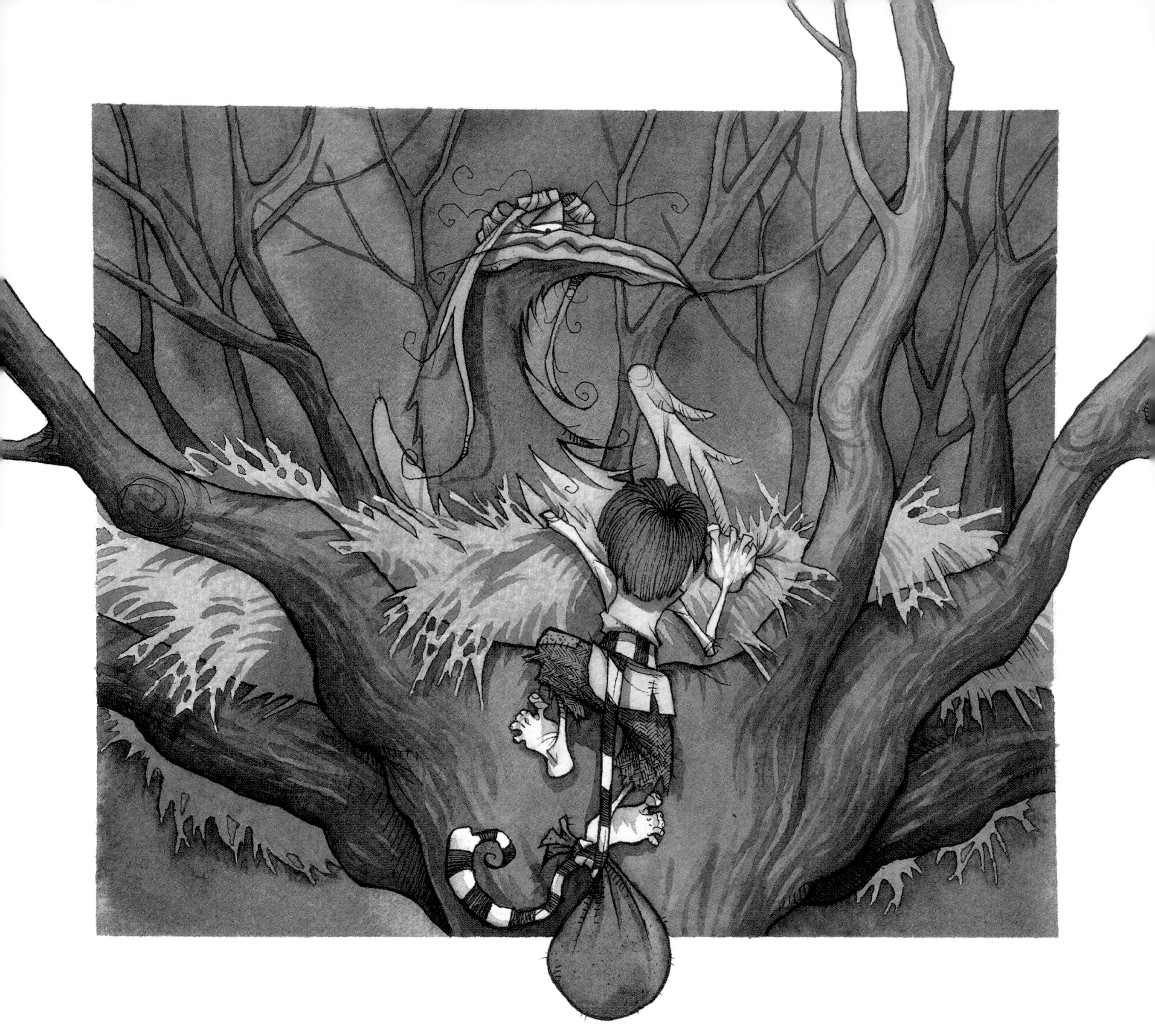

Little Jordan Ray sailed to where the nest lay
to retrieve the key in the egg on this October day.
He climbed the great oak to the nest drawing nigh,
where the griffin arose for a Reuben on rye.

"Why do you come up here with a sack on your back
in this midnight hour when I arise for a snack?"
asked the griffin as she shifted in her sack.

"I am sorry to be here so late in the day.
If you grant what I ask, then I'll be on my way.
I have here a mud-covered spud from the range
and all that I ask is your egg in exchange."

"My apologies lad, but I have no need for a spud.
Just a single spud all covered with mud."

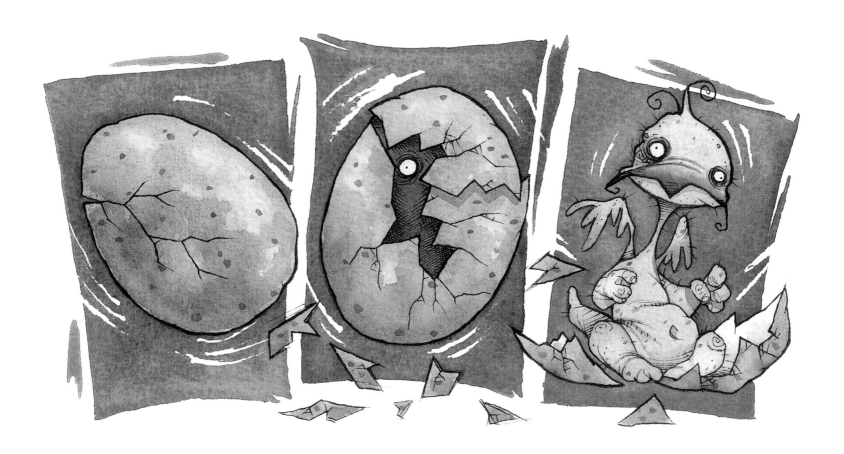

Then something happened, the spud began to crack.
Why it wasn't a spud at all, in the sack on his back.
A griffin hatched out of that muddy old spud.
This was the griffin's egg that was lost in the mud.

The birth of the child filled the griffin with glee.
She gave little Jordan Ray the egg with the key.

The key in the lock set the water nymph free.
She gave little Jordan Ray the sword of the sea.

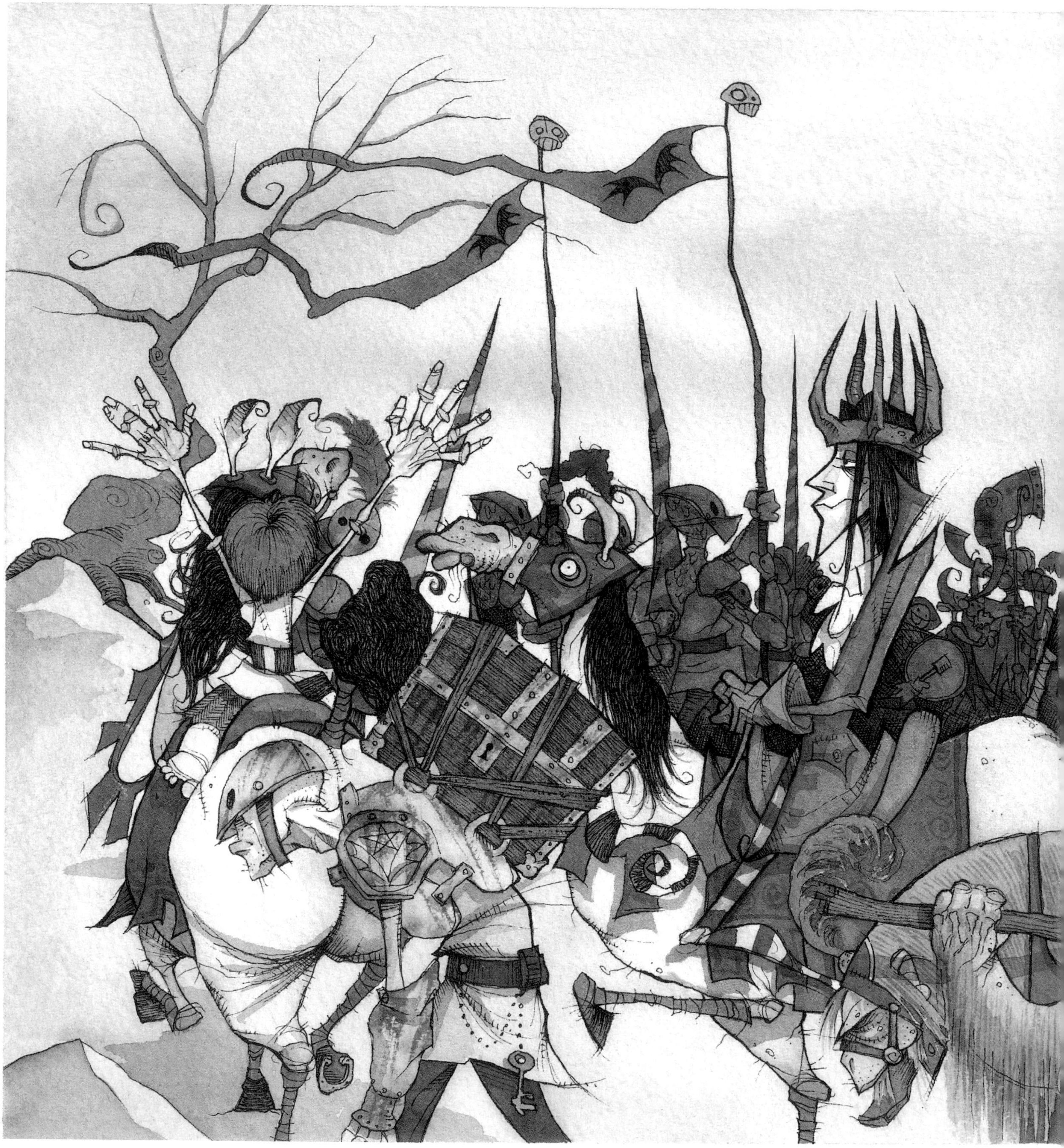

There was their son in ecstatic glee,
followed by the King and his noble army.
Hundreds of Knights, carrying silver and gold,
riding great steeds up the dirty old road.
There was the music of minstrels filling the air.
The parents just stood there, smiled and stared.

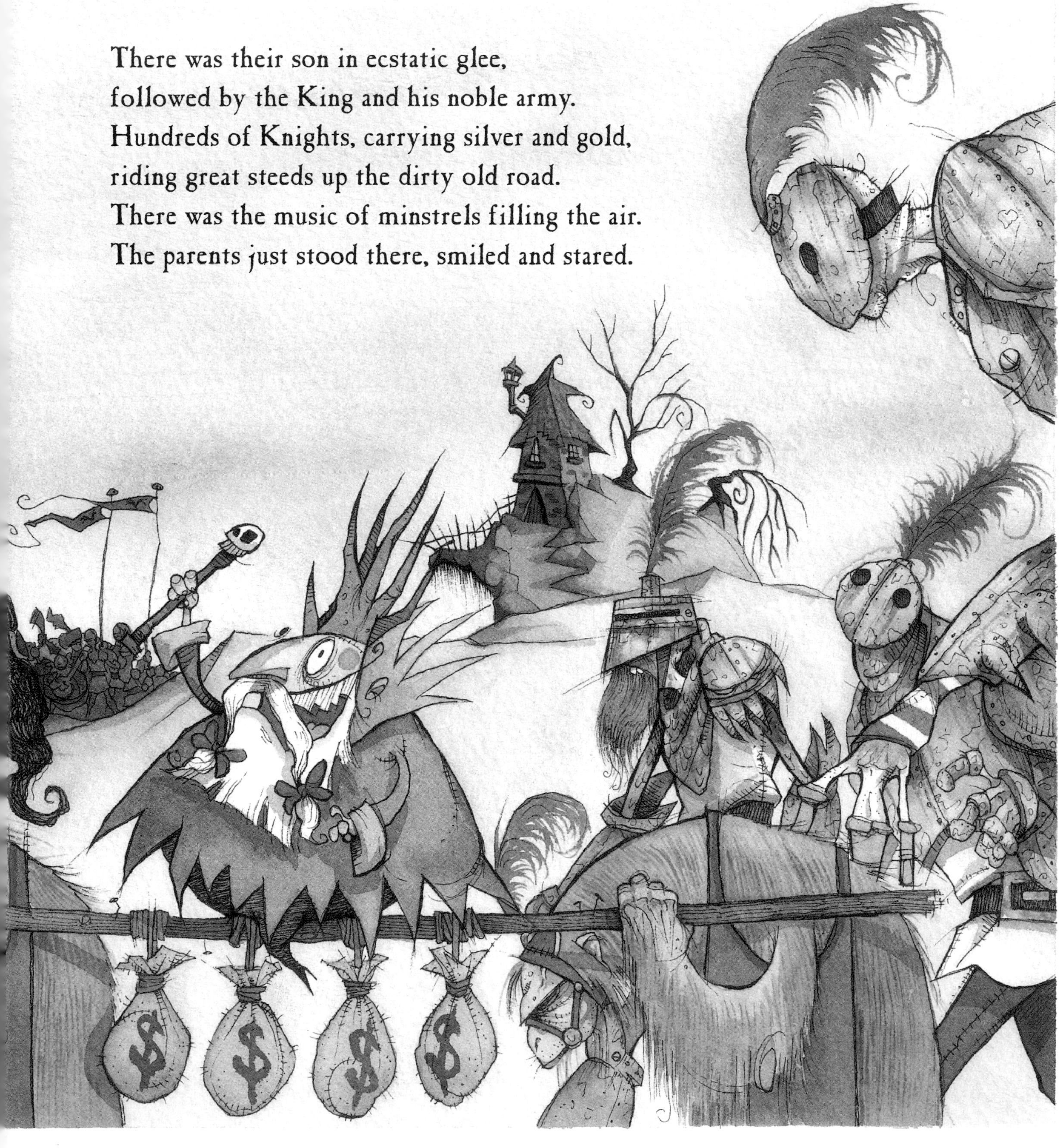

The boy ran up with his arms spread wide.
His parents squeezed him tight as they cried.
Little Jordan Ray lifted his head from a bow
"Mum and Dad, are you proud of me now?"

His folks replied, "We've always been proud of you.
But now," they added, "we are grateful too."

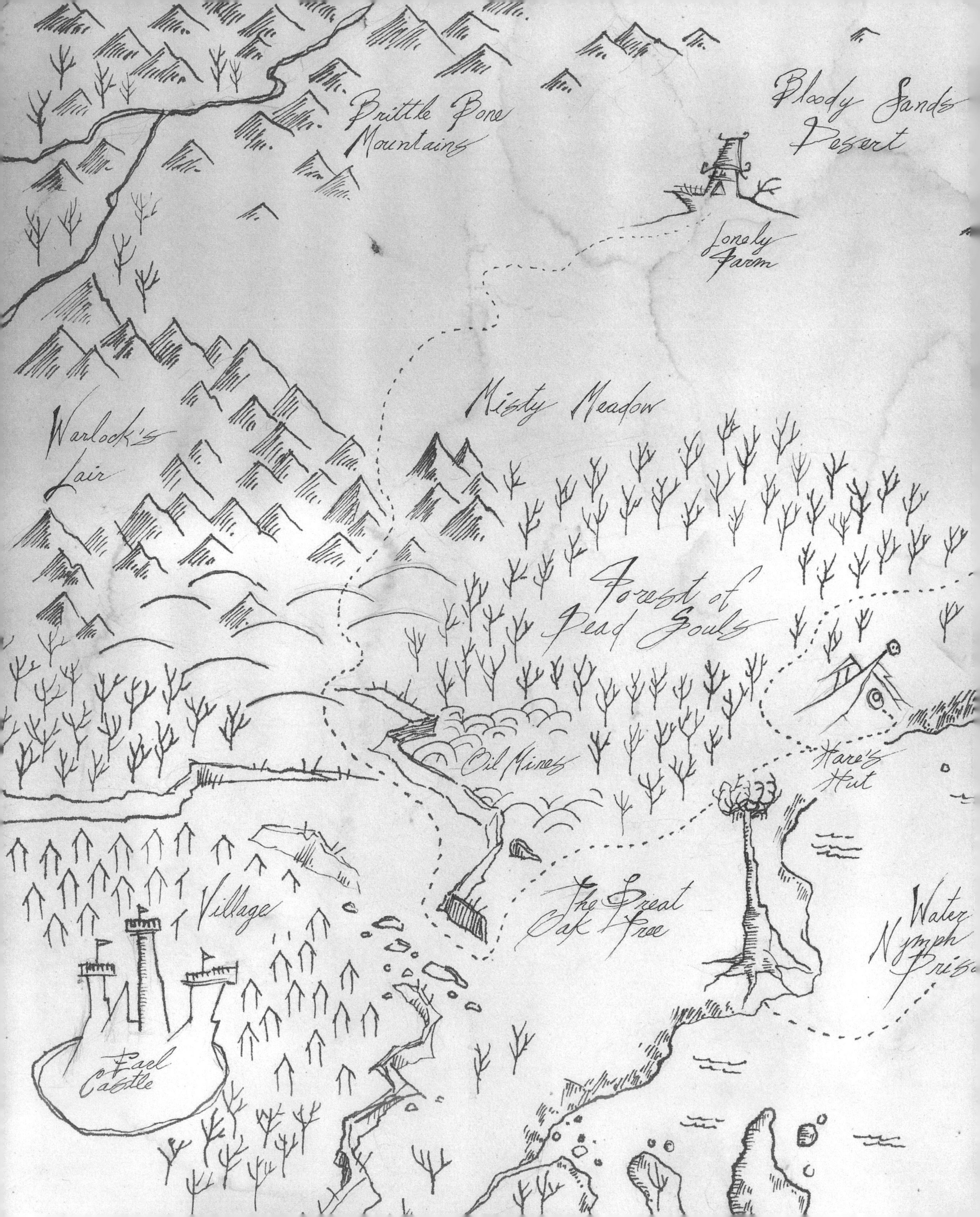
Brittle Bone Mountains
Bloody Sands Desert
Lonely Farm
Misty Meadow
Warlock's Lair
Forest of Dead Souls
Oil Mines
Hare's Hut
Village
The Great Oak Tree
Water Nymph Pris
Fael Castle